CHAPTER ONE

One fine day in Troll Village, Poppy sat out in front of her fuzzy pod, ready to teach the young Trolls surrounding her in a circle. They loved Queen Poppy, and they were excited to learn from her.

"Hooray for Queen Poppy!" shouted a little Troll named Keith. "Teach us something new!"

The other young Trolls took up the happy chant. "Teach us something new! Teach us

1

something new! Teach us something new!" They were so excited, they jumped up and started dancing in a conga line to the rhythm of their chanting. "Teach us something new!" *KICK!* "Teach us something new!" *KICK!*

Poppy grinned. She loved seeing the excited looks on the little Trolls' faces and hearing the amazement in their voices when she told them something they didn't know. She just *knew* they were going to love today's lesson. She'd planned a special surprise.

"Okay!" she said, gesturing for everyone to sit down again. They sat, but most were much too excited to sit *still,* so they wiggled and squirmed and bounced. "Today we've got a really fantastic treat. A guest speaker!"

"YAY!" the young Trolls cheered, even though most weren't exactly sure what a guest speaker was.

"Does anyone want to guess who our guest speaker is?" Poppy asked.

"Um, King Peppy?" asked one little girl Troll with bright purple hair.

"Nope," Poppy said, shaking her head. "That's an excellent guess, Jody, but it's not King Peppy. At least, not today. Maybe next time."

"King Gristle?" squeaked a tiny boy Troll named Rooty. Kings seemed to be a popular guess.

"No, not King Gristle, Rooty," Poppy said, smiling. "It'd be hard to hide him. You would probably already know if he was in the village."

The young Trolls nodded. That made sense. King Gristle was really big. They squinched up their faces, thinking hard. Who could the special guest be?

"Oh! I know! I know!" Keith said, waving his hand in the air frantically.

"Yes, Keith?" Poppy asked. "Who do you think our special guest speaker is?"

"Queen Poppy!" Keith said confidently.

Poppy looked confused. "Um, *I'm* Queen Poppy."

"I know!" Keith said. "Who could be a better guest speaker than you?"

Laughing, she said, "Thank you! But our guest speaker isn't Queen Poppy, or King

Peppy, or King Gristle." She got to her feet and gestured toward the nearest tree. "No, today it is our honor to welcome our very special guest speaker . . . GUY DIAMOND!"

"Yay!" cheered the young Trolls, hopping and dancing around. They clapped and whistled as Guy Diamond popped into their circle from behind the tree and took a bow.

"Thank you, thank you! Thank you very much!" said the friendly Troll in his shimmery voice. He shone and sparkled as though he'd been dipped in silver glitter from head to toe. His bluish-white hair stood straight up, doubling his height. And his handsome wide nose was as green as the strap on his Hug Time watch. "It's great to be here today! I'm so glad Queen Poppy invited me to be your special guest speaker!"

"So," Poppy said as she settled down to listen, "please tell us what you're going to talk about today, Guy Diamond."

"All right," Guy said, standing with his feet apart and his fists on his hips. "First, a quick question. Does anyone here like . . . HOLIDAYS?" Guy's voice hit three different notes, and the little Trolls went wild.

"Me!" "Me!" "I do, I do!" they shouted. As Guy knew very well, ALL Trolls loved holidays!

"Well," he continued, "today I'm going to tell you about a very special holiday! Can anyone guess what it is?"

The young Trolls thought hard.

"Naked Day?" guessed one.

"Burp Day?" suggested another.

"The Solar Equinox?" ventured a particularly clever young Troll.

Guy was impressed by all the guesses. "Nope. Those are fantastic holidays, but I'm here to talk about my personal favorite holiday, THE RAINBOW RAVE! Who here likes rainbows?"

A forest of hands shot into the air. "Me!" "Me!" "I LOVE rainbows!"

Guy nodded. "I totally agree. One hundred percent. Rainbows are terrific. Never met one I didn't love. What do you like about them?"

"The bright colors!" Jody cried.

"The way they hang in the sky!" Rooty yelled.

"The way they demonstrate the refraction of

sunlight by drops of water in the atmosphere," stated the clever young Troll, whose name was Leif. The other Trolls turned and stared at him.

"Dude," Keith said. "I'm not sure you belong in this class."

Leif nodded, considering. He thought perhaps Keith was right. . . .

Guy Diamond smiled. "I love all those things about rainbows, too. Most of the time when we see a rainbow in the sky, there's only one. Maybe two. But there's one special day of the year when the sky is FULL of rainbows! All the conditions are just right for the sky to fill up with lots and lots of rainbows. You'll see them everywhere you look! It's like a natural fireworks display—only during the day. While the sun is shining! Way before your bedtime!"

"Does it rain?" a small girl Troll named Twiggie asked.

"No!" Guy answered. "It doesn't even rain! The sun is shining, but the sky's full of rainbows! And on that special day, we celebrate the rainbows with a Rainbow Rave!"

"Yay!" Keith cheered. "Um, what's a Rainbow Rave?"

Guy explained that during a Rainbow Rave, Trolls spend the whole day celebrating rainbows with all kinds of fun activities. They sing songs about rainbows. They dress up as rainbows. They eat cupcakes frosted with rainbow icing. They style their hair into rainbows. And they dance the Rainbow, lining up by color in an arc

that stretches through the village. As an enthusiastic dancer, Guy was especially fond of that
activity.

Jody raised her hand. "Um, Mr. Diamond,
I have a question."

"Yes?" Guy said.

"When is the next Rainbow Rave?"

Looking serious, Guy pretended to think
hard about the answer. "Let's see, when is the
next Rainbow Rave? After all, the conditions
have to be exactly right. Hmm. Oh, that's right.
The next Rainbow Rave is . . . TOMORROW!"

The little Trolls sat for a second, stunned by
the sensational news. Then they leapt to their
feet, squealing and cheering! The very next day,
every Troll in Troll Village would celebrate

at the Rainbow Rave! Needless to say, Queen Poppy's guest speaker was a big hit.

That night, most of the young Trolls were so excited, they could hardly sleep a wink. (Except Leif, who knew the importance of getting at least eight hours of sleep every night.)

Guy couldn't sleep, either. He lay in bed in his glittery pod with his eyes wide open, wiggling his toes, thinking about the next day's festivities. Around midnight, he decided to get up and take a short walk, hoping to tire himself out so he could fall asleep and be rested for the big day.

The moon was full. As Guy strolled through the quiet village, he sparkled in the bright silvery moonlight. Looking up, he studied the night sky. To him, the conditions looked perfect. He was sure the next day would be one of the finest Rainbow Raves anyone had ever seen. Satisfied, he went back inside his pod, climbed into bed, and quickly fell asleep, dreaming of the perfect Rainbow Rave.

But the next morning, when Guy woke early and rushed out to see all the rainbows in the sky, he was shocked.

THERE WASN'T A SINGLE RAINBOW!

CHAPTER TWO

Guy couldn't believe it. Where were all the rainbows? The sky over Troll Village should have been full of them!

He stood there, staring, his mouth hanging wide open in disbelief. Then he thought maybe the rainbows would suddenly start popping into the sky one by one.

But they didn't. The sky was blue, the sun was shining, and there were a few puffy white clouds drifting by—but no rainbows.

Guy headed toward the center of Troll Village to see if anyone knew what was going on. As he hurried along, the first Troll he met was Branch, who was gathering sticks.

"Branch!" Guy asked breathlessly. "Where are all the rainbows?"

"Usually in the sky," Branch answered matter-of-factly. "Oh, and on Poppy's invitations. I'm surprised you didn't already know that, Guy."

"No," Guy explained. "I KNOW rainbows are usually in the sky. But this is the day of the Rainbow Rave, and there are supposed to be *dozens* of rainbows up there!"

Branch looked up. He'd completely forgotten about the Rainbow Rave, so he hadn't even noticed that the rainbows were missing.

"Hmm," he said. "You're right. Not a single rainbow. Clouds, yes. Rainbows, no."

"I TOLD you!" Guy said.

"Are you sure this is the right day?" Branch asked. "Maybe the Rainbow Rave's supposed to be tomorrow. Or maybe we missed it."

Guy couldn't believe what he was hearing. "MISSED it? How could we possibly miss it? It's one of the most fantastic days there is!"

Branch nodded slowly. "You're right. We wouldn't miss it. It's way too colorful." He thought a moment. Then he got an idea. "Maybe the rainbows are missing because of some kind of deep, dark conspiracy!"

Guy looked puzzled. "Conspiracy? By whom?"

"Secret anti-rainbow forces, of course," Branch explained, lowering his voice and looking around to see who might be eavesdropping. "A powerful group of rainbow haters working together to ruin our rave! It makes complete sense when you think about it."

Guy thought about it, but it didn't make complete sense to him. It didn't even make partial sense. Why would anyone be against rainbows? They were so pretty!

"Okay, well, that's one theory," Guy said politely. "I think maybe I'll go see if anyone else knows what happened to all the rainbows."

"Fine," Branch shrugged. "But I'm sure

you'll find it's all a big conspiracy. It always is."

As Guy headed on through the village, he spotted Biggie coming out of the bakery with a big tray full of cupcakes. They were frosted with rainbow icing and dusted with rainbow sprinkles. Guy hurried over to him.

"Good morning, Biggie!" Guy said. "Happy Rainbow Rave!"

"Happy Rainbow Rave!" Biggie answered cheerfully as he set the tray down on a table he'd set up outside. "I've got the rainbow cupcakes all ready! Have one! Or two! There are plenty!"

The cupcakes looked delicious—and beautiful, with their colorful icing. Guy was tempted. But this was no time to enjoy sweets. They had a crisis to confront! A mystery to solve!

"No, thank you," Guy said. "They look delicious, but I'm too worried about the rainbows!"

"What rainbows?" Biggie asked, puzzled.

"Exactly!" Guy said, flinging his arms out. "Where are all the rainbows? The sky's supposed to be full of them!"

Biggie looked up. He'd been so busy getting his rainbow cupcakes ready that he hadn't had a chance to study the sky.

"Hey," he said, "where are the rainbows?"

"That's what *I'd* like to know!" Guy said.

Biggie's lip started to quiver. "But if there aren't any rainbows," he asked, his voice choked with emotion, "how are we supposed to have a Rainbow Rave?"

"I don't know," Guy admitted.

They both stood there for a moment, staring sadly up at the sky. Then Biggie looked hopeful. "Hey, maybe they're just late!" he suggested. "Maybe they overslept!"

Guy looked doubtful. "I don't think rainbows sleep. But maybe you're right. Maybe they'll show up a little later this morning."

But as the morning went on, no rainbows appeared in the sky. The Trolls went ahead and put up their decorations anyway, getting ready for their rainbow dances and rainbow games. Every few minutes, they'd sneak another glance at the sky, hoping the rainbows were there.

But they weren't.

The young Trolls Guy had talked to the day

before were especially disappointed. They'd really been looking forward to the Rainbow Rave. When they saw Guy, they surrounded him, jumping up and down and bombarding him with questions.

"Mr. Diamond, where are the rainbows?"

"What happened to them?"

"Are they still coming?"

As Guy was trying to think of what to say, Poppy hurried over.

"Guy!" she said. "Thanks again for your terrific talk yesterday! That was awesome!"

"Yeah, it was awesome," Keith agreed. "But the rainbows not showing up today is NOT awesome!"

"TOTALLY not awesome!" said Rooty.

Even though Poppy was worried about the rainbows not being there for the Rainbow Rave, she smiled, determined that everyone was going to have a good time anyway. "Don't worry! We've got cupcakes and dances and songs and games. We're going to have a fabulous day even if the rainbows don't show up! Which they will! Eventually. I'm pretty sure. . . ."

The young Trolls looked uncertain.

"It seems kind of weird to have a Rainbow Rave with no rainbows," Twiggie said. The others nodded.

Secretly, Guy agreed. He didn't want to say it out loud, but without a sky full of rainbows, what was the point of singing songs about rainbows and dancing the Rainbow? It just wouldn't be the same. The magical thing about the Rainbow Rave was celebrating under a sky full of bright, shining rainbows. Without them . . .

"I saw something," said a voice behind Guy. "I think the rainbows were TAKEN!"

CHAPTER THREE

Guy spun around. He saw Karma, the Troll who loved nature more than any other Troll. She had leaves and sticks wound into her green hair, and she wore a skirt the color of sunshine.

"What did you say?" Guy asked.

"I said I saw something," Karma repeated. "Something that makes me think maybe the rainbows were taken!"

The little Trolls, Poppy, and Guy gasped. Who would *take* rainbows on the day of the

Rainbow Rave? What a terrible thought!

Poppy rushed over to Karma. "What did you see, Karma? Tell us!"

"Well," she began, "early this morning, just as the sun was coming up, I was walking in the woods, when—"

FWEE FWEE DEE DEE DWEEEE FWEE DOODLY DOOOO! Suddenly, loud music drowned out Karma's story. The Trolls looked around to see where it was coming from. Cooper strolled up to the group, blowing into his harmonica. *FWEE DOODLY DEEDLE DEEE!*

"COOPER!" Poppy shouted, startling the four-legged Troll with the long neck. He stopped playing his harmonica.

"Oh, hi, Poppy! Hi, Guy Diamond! Hi,

Karma! Happy Rainbow Rave! I was just practicing a new song I wrote for our celebration. It's called 'Rainbows Are the Rainbowiest Bows Made out of Rain!'" Cooper said. He looked around conspiratorially, then whispered, "It's about rainbows."

"That's wonderful, Cooper," Poppy said, "but in case you haven't noticed, there aren't any rainbows in the sky."

"Really?" Cooper said, surprised. "I was too busy working on my new song to check out the sky." He looked up, craning his long neck all around. Then he looked back at his fellow Trolls. "You're right! No rainbows! On the day of the Rainbow Rave! What happened to them?"

Guy shrugged. "We don't know, Cooper. But

Karma saw something this morning that makes her think somebody *took* the rainbows!"

Cooper's eyes grew wide. "Took?" He turned to Karma. "What was it, Karma? What did you see? WHY WON'T YOU TELL US?"

Leif tugged on Cooper's leg. "Excuse me, Mr. Cooper, but I can explain. Ms. Karma was about to tell us what she saw when you came in playing your harmonica. Your music drowned her out, so she stopped speaking. Now that you've finished playing, at least for the moment, she'll be able to resume her fascinating story."

Everyone stared at the little Troll.

Cooper bent his long neck down until his head was close to the clever young Troll's face. "You are very smart! Thank you for that excellent explanation," Cooper told him.

"You're welcome," said Leif. "I liked your song."

"Thank you!" Cooper said. "It's a work in progress." He turned to Karma, who had picked a flower and was tying it into her hair next to several others. "Karma, I'm sorry I interrupted your story. Please continue!"

Karma smiled. "Oh, no problem, Cooper! Anyway, as I was saying, early this morning, just as the sun was coming up, I was walking in the woods, when—"

Branch came running up. "Did someone say something about the rainbows being stolen? That's GOTTA be part of a big conspiracy, right? What'd I tell you, Guy? CONSPIRACY!"

"Where? WHERE?" Cooper asked, wheeling around, afraid a big, mean conspiracy was about to jump on him.

Poppy held her hands up and patted the air. "Okay, everybody," she said in a soothing voice. "Let's all just take a deep breath, calm down, and listen to what Karma has to say. Karma?"

Karma was now down on all fours, staring at a tiny critter she'd noticed digging a hole in the ground. She looked up. "Hmm?" she said. "Oh, right! My story!" She stood up, not bothering to brush the dirt off her hands and knees. "Okay! As I was saying—early this morning, just as the sun was coming up, I was walking in the woods. I love that time of day, when all the critters are waking up, and stretching, and starting to sing."

The other Trolls nodded. Though some of them liked to sleep late, they still knew what Karma was talking about. They all liked the sounds of nature first thing in the morning.

Karma fiddled with a stick in her hair. "I thought maybe I'd find some special flowers to put in my hair. And some sticks. And rocks. Maybe a little dirt."

Some of the young Trolls looked puzzled. They thought they were supposed to keep their hair really clean so it would shine in the light. They'd never heard of putting dirt in their hair. A couple of them made mental notes to try it later.

"I'd found some flowers that I liked and was thinking about heading back into the village,"

Karma continued. "But then I saw something through the trees. It was just a quick glimpse, but I'm pretty sure I saw someone hurrying away, dragging a bunch of rainbows!"

Branch frowned. "Are you sure you saw just one Troll? Not a group of Trolls? Like in a conspiracy? Or was it something other than a Troll?"

Karma thought for a moment, then shook her head. "Nope. Not a group. A someone. But there were lots of rainbows!"

Guy Diamond felt sure that Karma had seen a rainbow thief. If they could just catch the thief, maybe they could get the rainbows back and the Rainbow Rave would be saved! "What did this someone look like?" he asked urgently.

Karma twirled some of her green hair around a finger. "Well, like I said, it was just a glimpse. And he was partially blocked by all the rainbows he was dragging."

"But it was a he?" Poppy said. "A guy took the rainbows?"

"I *think* so," Karma said, nodding slowly.

"Let's start with the most important thing," Poppy suggested. "What was his hair like?"

"I'm not sure he *had* hair," Karma answered.

They all gasped. No hair?

"I guess he *might* have had hair," Karma went on. "I didn't really get a good look at him through the trees."

"Well, if he *did* have hair," Poppy said, "what color was it?"

Karma thought a moment. "Um, white. But it wasn't hair, exactly. More like . . . puffs."

"White puffs?" Branch said, puzzled. "Wait a minute. . . . Did this guy have skinny arms and legs? With a fluffy body? Striped gym socks with no shoes?"

"Yes!" Karma agreed, nodding. "He did!"

Branch and Guy turned to each other. "Cloud Guy!" they said at the same time.

"But why would Cloud Guy steal all the rainbows?" Poppy asked.

That was a good question. Guy Diamond had no idea why Cloud Guy would steal the rainbows and ruin the Trolls' Rainbow Rave.

But he intended to find out.

CHAPTER FOUR

"I'm going to find Cloud Guy and ask him why he stole all the rainbows!" Guy Diamond said, turning and heading into the woods.

"Wait a minute, Guy," Poppy said reasonably. "We don't know for sure that Cloud Guy stole the rainbows."

"Fine," Guy said. "I'm going to go ask him IF he stole the rainbows!"

"Or borrowed them," Poppy said.

"Or borrowed them," Guy agreed. "Now, where exactly does Cloud Guy live?"

The Trolls looked at each other. Though they'd *met* Cloud Guy, they weren't sure where he lived. He was kind of mysterious. It seemed as though he just showed up every once in a while. But nobody had ever visited him at his house. No one knew if he even *had* a house.

Branch stepped forward. "Well, the first time Poppy and I saw Cloud Guy, he looked like he was up in the sky. Like, you know, a cloud. But then he walked down the side of a tree."

"Okay," Guy Diamond said slowly. "Where was this tree?"

"Right by the escape-route tunnels that lead to the old Troll Tree in Bergen Town," Poppy said. "He welcomed us to the tunnels and knew all about them, so maybe he lives around there. Or at least visits a lot."

"Does he seem like the kind of fellow who would take rainbows?" Guy asked.

"No," Poppy said, shaking her head. "Definitely not. He was nice. Kind of goofy, but nice. And I don't think he said anything about rainbows."

"Well," Branch objected. "He wasn't *that* nice. Before he would help us, he insisted that I give him a high five!"

Poppy giggled. Branch glared at her. She put on a serious face.

"I'll give you a little hint about dealing with Cloud Guy," Branch said, putting his arm around Guy's shoulders and taking him aside. "If you really want him to tell you something, show him a nice, sharp stick. That'll get his attention."

"A sharp stick?" Guy asked, puzzled. "You mean, like, to poke him with?"

"I never poked him with it," Branch insisted. "But if he *thought* I was going to poke him with the stick . . . well, that was his misunderstanding. Anyway, it got him to show us which tunnel led to the old Troll Tree. And fast, too. He ran the whole way."

"Thanks for the tip," Guy said. "I'll keep it in mind." Guy had no intention of threatening anyone with a pointy stick, even if he—or she—did turn out to be a rainbow thief. He took a deep breath. "It's a pretty long way to the escape-route tunnels, so I'd better hurry up if I'm going to get the rainbows back in the sky before the day is over." He started walking briskly toward the path leading out of Troll Village. "And I am! I'm sure of it!"

"Wait!" Poppy cried after him. "You're not going all alone, are you?"

Guy turned back. "I don't mind. I think everyone else should stay here and get everything ready for the Rainbow Rave so the young Trolls won't be disappointed."

Poppy looked at the group of youngsters. It would be a shame to let them down. If the rest of the Trolls worked together while Guy went looking for Cloud Guy, they could make a fun day for the little Trolls full of cupcakes, songs, and dancing.

But she still didn't like the idea of Guy going off into the woods by himself. She'd done that herself once, and it had been pretty dangerous.

Then Poppy got an idea. She spotted DJ Suki on the other side of the village square. "DJ Suki!" she called. "Can I talk to you for a minute?"

"Sure, Poppy!" DJ Suki called back, hurrying across the square. "What's up, Buttercup?"

"How are your preparations for the Rainbow Rave dance?" Poppy asked. "Have you got your Wooferbug and Be-bop Bugs ready?"

"Yup!" DJ Suki said. "We're all ready to go! Just cue the music and we'll start the jams!"

"Great!" Poppy said. "So you're free to run

a little errand with Guy Diamond?"

DJ Suki grinned. "Sure! Guy and I make a great team. The DJ and the Dancer!"

Smiling, Guy did a little spin, ending with his hands out. "Great idea, Poppy! Come on, DJ Suki, let's get going. I'll tell you all about it on the way."

"Good luck!" Poppy said. "And be careful! It can get kind of weird out there in the forest."

The two Trolls hurried out of Troll Village and into the woods. As they went, Guy told DJ Suki about the missing rainbows, and Cloud Guy, and the old escape-route tunnels.

"How far is it to the tunnels?" DJ Suki asked as they rushed past huge trees and multicolored flowers.

"I'm not sure," Guy admitted. "But I think it's pretty far."

"Then we'd better run," DJ Suki suggested. "We've got to get the rainbows back before the Rainbow Rave is over!"

"Right!" Guy agreed.

They broke into a run, but it wasn't long before they both had to stop. Breathing hard, they leaned over, resting their hands on their knees.

"Something tells me," DJ Suki said, panting, "we're not going to be able to run the whole way."

"I . . . agree . . . ," Guy gasped. "Time to let our hair do the walking!"

DJ Suki smiled. "Right! We'll hair-swing through the trees!"

"As long as there are branches—and there seem to be plenty—we should be fine," Guy said. "Ready?"

"Ready!"

They both jumped up and shot their long hair forward until it wrapped around a branch. They swung out, and when they were almost as far as they could go, they released their hair and whipped it ahead to the next branch. In this way, they zoomed through the woods much faster than they could have walked or even run.

Swinging by their hair was not only fast, it was a wonderful way to travel. Fresh air blew against their skin as they sped from branch to branch. "WHOO-HOOOO!" DJ Suki whooped as she shot through the air.

"YEEEAAAHHHH!" Guy Diamond shouted, zipping along next to her.

They were having a great time, but they didn't realize that creatures in the dark forest could hear their whooping and shouting. And not all of those creatures were friendly.

CHAPTER FIVE

Guy Diamond flew through the air, aiming his bluish-white hair at the next branch. *THWAP!* His hair hit the limb and wrapped around it. He jerked his head, pulling himself forward. DJ Suki did the same thing right next to him. They sailed from tree to tree, loving the sensation of speed, until—

ZAP! CRACK! One gnarled branch broke and fell! Because their hair was wrapped around it, Guy and DJ Suki were pulled down.

"YAAAAHHHH!" they screamed as they plummeted toward the ground.

"UNWIND!" Guy shouted.

With a nimble twist and jerk of their heads, the two Trolls unwound their hair from the branch before it hit the ground. Then they slammed their hair into the dirt like rigid poles and slid down, spinning around the hair poles like firefighters and landing without a scratch.

"Whew!" DJ Suki said, unwinding her hair. "That was close! What happened to the branch? Why did it break?"

They smelled an odd scent, like something was burning. The broken end of the branch was smoking a little.

"Did the branch get hit by lightning?" Guy

asked, sniffing. "It smells like smoke."

"Lightning? How?" DJ Suki asked as they walked closer to the smoking end of the limb. She held out her hand with the palm up. "It's not raining. And the sun's still shining. There's not a cloud in the sky!"

"You're right," Guy said, puzzled. "But just before the branch broke, I thought I heard a—"

ZAP!

"Wow," DJ Suki said. "That's the most realistic imitation of a zap I've ever heard. How did you do that?"

"I didn't! That wasn't me!" Guy said, looking around. "That was an actual—"

ZAP! A little bolt of energy hit the ground near them.

"Where are these zaps coming from?" DJ Suki shouted.

"There!" Guy yelled, pointing. "It's a Zapperzine! RUN!"

The Zapperzine was a fierce, fuzzy creature with bulging eyes, a long neck, and four short legs. In the middle of its forehead was a pointy bright-green zapper. It ran toward the Trolls, shooting mini bolts from its zapper. *ZAP! ZAP! ZAP!*

Luckily, the Zapperzine couldn't run very fast. It had to keep stopping to aim its zapper. But it could shoot blasts of energy pretty far. The Trolls zigged and zagged, making it harder for the Zapperzine to zap them. Whenever they could, they ran behind boulders, tree stumps, and mushrooms, putting obstacles between them and the Zapperzine.

"Go! Go! Go!" Guy urged DJ Suki, but she didn't need much urging. She'd never been zapped by a Zapperzine, and she was pretty sure she wouldn't like it.

As they ran, they noticed that the woods were thinning out. There weren't so many trees and bushes. Ahead of them lay a wide, flat open space.

"We can't run that way!" Guy wailed. "There's nothing to hide behind! We'll be easy targets for the Zapperzine!"

"There's nowhere else to go!" DJ Suki said. "We can't turn around and run back toward that thing. It'll zap us for sure!"

ZAP! ZAP! ZAP! The Zapperzine fired off three bolts that hit the ground WAY too close to the running Trolls! They could feel the air crackle around them with hot energy, and they smelled something burning.

With no choice but to go forward, Guy and DJ Suki ran out into the open field. As they ran, they could still hear the zapping, but the sounds seemed to be farther away. Guy looked back over his shoulder.

"Look!" he said. "The Zapperzine's not following us anymore!"

DJ Suki looked back, too. The Zapperzine had stopped right at the edge of the field. The bug heaved a disappointed sigh, turned around, and disappeared into the dark woods.

"That's weird," DJ Suki said. "I wonder why it stopped chasing us."

"Maybe it had to go recharge," Guy suggested.

"Maybe," DJ Suki said doubtfully. "But it was still trying to zap us right up to the moment it stopped following us, almost like it was afraid to come out onto this open ground."

They'd stopped to catch their breath. Guy looked around. "What's to be afraid of?" he asked. "There's nothing here."

DJ Suki shrugged. "I don't know. Maybe it's just too—"

BLOOOOSH! Just a few feet ahead of them, a geyser of mud shot into the sky!

"WHAAAAAH!" they screamed.

The mud fell back to the ground, and the

hole it had shot out of disappeared. The ground looked perfectly smooth, as though nothing had happened.

"I do NOT want to step on top of one of those," DJ Suki said. "It would dull all my glitter!" She was wearing her usual striped knit pants and top, a pair of bracelets, and a jewel in her belly button.

"I don't want to step on one of those things, either," Guy agreed, "even though I don't have to worry about getting my clothes muddy. But how are we supposed to know where they are?"

"I don't know," DJ Suki said. "The whole field looks flat. Let's just stand here a second and see if it happens again."

"Okay," Guy agreed, taking a big breath to

calm himself. "Good idea." They stood still, waiting.

Nothing happened.

Guy shrugged. "Maybe the mud geyser only happens once a da—"

BLORRSSSHHH! A few steps ahead of them, another fountain of mud shot into the sky! This one went even higher than the first one, sending more mud into the air. But like the first geyser, once the mud fell back down, there was no sign that it had ever erupted.

Guy and DJ Suki froze, afraid to take another step and risk being blasted up on a column of mud.

"What are we going to do?" Guy whispered, worried his voice might trigger another muddy explosion.

"I noticed something just before that geyser burst," DJ Suki said quietly.

"What?" Guy asked, eager for any information that might help them escape from this frightening field.

"It was like a little hissing sound," she explained. "My eyes went to the spot on the ground where I heard the hissing. And then I saw a tiny bump in the dirt, like a small bulge, just before the geyser blew."

Guy nodded. "Now that you mention it, I think I heard that hissing, too! Maybe if we listen really carefully, and watch for little bumps, we can avoid the mud jets and get across this field!"

They both crouched down, keeping their ears low, and started slowly creeping toward the opposite side of the field. *Hissssss . . .*

"There!" DJ Suki said, pointing right in front of them, where a tiny bump rose from the ground. The Trolls jumped to the side, getting as far away from the bump as they could.

BLOOOOOSHHH! The powerful mud geyser shot into the air, but the Trolls weren't standing on it when it erupted.

Listening and staring at the ground, they cautiously crept across the field, avoiding the mud geysers each time they blew.

Hisssss . . . BLORRRSSH!

Hissss . . . KA-BLOYSSSHHH!

Hisss . . . SHPLOOOOSSSHP!

After what seemed like hours (but was really only a few minutes), they stepped onto green moss and grass, finally off the explosive field.

"We made it!" they cried, hugging joyfully.

"Mud-free!" added DJ Suki.

And there were trees again! The two Trolls smiled at each other and, without having to say a word, shot their hair up to a branch and swung themselves forward.

This time, though, they didn't whoop.

CHAPTER SIX

But the trees didn't last forever. As Guy Diamond and DJ Suki made their way to the escape-route tunnels to look for Cloud Guy, they entered patches of land where the trees were too far apart to swing between. Then the Trolls had to drop to the ground and walk as quickly as they could.

"How much farther?" DJ Suki asked.

"I think we're getting close," Guy said.

CLICK-CLICK! CLICK-CLICK!

DJ Suki looked around. "What was that?"

"What was what?"

"That clicking sound! Didn't you hear it?"

"Yes," Guy said. "But I thought it was you.
You're always hearing music in your head, so
I thought maybe you were just snapping your
fingers."

"It wasn't me."

Guy pointed. "It was . . . THAT!"

Something was crawling out from under
a rock. Covered in bright purple and yellow
stripes, it had two long pincers that it was
waving and snapping. *CLICK-CLICK! CLICK-
CLICK!* On the end of its tail, which curved up
over its back until it reached out in front of its

head, was a third sharp pincer. That snapped open and closed, too. *CLICK-CLICK!* From head to tail, it was more than twice as long as the Trolls were tall.

"A Pinchmalla!" DJ Suki cried.

"I do NOT want to be pinched by those pincers!" Guy declared.

"Me neither!" DJ Suki agreed. "RUN!"

They ran toward the nearest tree, hoping they could shoot their hair up onto a branch and swing away to safety. But before they could reach the tree, two more Pinchmallas skittered out from under rocks and blocked their path! The Trolls skidded to a stop.

They were surrounded by the three snapping Pinchmallas.

CLICK-CLICK! CLICK-CLICK! CLICK-CLICK!

The Pinchmallas slowly closed in on DJ Suki and Guy, clacking the pincers on their front legs and tails. The Trolls stood back-to-back with their hands held out in front of them urgently, hoping the Pinchmallas would stop. And turn around. And go away.

They didn't. They just kept coming.

When the three Pinchmallas were only a few steps from the Trolls, Guy clapped his hands together, rubbed them vigorously, and blew on them. *POOF!*

Glitter flew into the face of the closest Pinchmalla. It swiped at its eyes with its pincers, trying to wipe away the glitter.

Before the other two Pinchmallas could react, Guy clapped his hands together again and rubbed his palms like crazy. *POOF! POOF!* He blew clouds of silvery glitter right into the faces of the other two Pinchmallas.

EEERRREEEERRR! shrieked the Pinchmallas as they wiped their faces. Before they could clean off all the glitter, Guy grabbed DJ Suki's hand and ran past the beasts.

"Come on!" he yelled. "Before they get the glitter off!"

They sprinted as fast as their legs could carry them. When they were close enough to a tree branch, they whipped their hair up and around the limb and rocketed off!

Unfortunately, the Trolls could only swing

on a few branches before the trees were too far apart again. But when they looked back, no Pinchmallas were following them.

"Great work with your glitter, Guy!" DJ Suki enthused. "Those Pinchmallas never knew what hit them! You saved us from a lot of painful pinches!"

"How did you know those were Pinchmallas?" Guy asked. "Had you seen them before?"

DJ Suki shrugged. "Nope. But I'd heard about them from Karma. She'd seen a couple when she was out exploring the forest. She was excited about it. I think she actually *likes* them!"

Guy smiled. "As long as it's part of nature, Karma likes it."

"It's all beautiful until someone gets pinched!" DJ Suki said.

While they were talking, they walked into another small clump of trees.

"Do you want to hair-swing again? It's faster," DJ Suki pointed out.

"Sure," Guy said. "That sounds like a good ide—"

WHAP!

A leafy branch slapped the ground right next to them! But it hadn't fallen off the tree, because it rose back up and then came down again—this time even closer to where they were standing!

SLAP!

"What is going on?" DJ Suki asked.

"I'm not sure," Guy answered, "but I think

that tree branch just tried to *swat* us!"

WHAP! Another leafy branch swatted the ground. The Trolls took off running, dodging as the trees tried to squish them with their branches. Luckily, as dancers, they had lots of good moves and were quick on their feet.

"I really don't understand why Karma loves nature so much!" DJ Suki shouted as they sprinted through the woods, jumping and rolling out of the way of the slapping branches. "Give me music every time! It's so much less DANGEROUS!"

Guy agreed, though he was too busy running and avoiding the branches to say so. He kept looking up to see where the branches were, but then he'd trip over things on the ground, like stones and roots. That turned out to be lucky whenever he tripped and rolled out of the way just as another limb covered in leaves came swatting down.

WHAP! SWAT!

"That way!" DJ Suki yelled. "We're almost out from under these Swat Trees!"

"I never heard of Swat Trees!" Guy gasped.

"That's because I just made that name up!" DJ Suki said, sprinting for the edge of the small cluster of nasty trees. When the Trolls saw an open meadow beyond them, they both dove for it, escaping just as two more huge branches slapped the ground. *WHOMMMMPPP! WHOMMMMPPPP!*

They sat on the grass for a moment, catching

their breath, looking back at the woods they'd just run through. It looked perfectly peaceful, with no branches slapping down. They even heard a Chimer singing.

"Man," DJ Suki admitted, "I don't know how much more of this I can take!"

Guy looked around and spotted something on the other side of the meadow.

"Look!" he said, pointing. "See those caves? I think those are the openings to the escape-route tunnels. Come on! We're almost there!"

Knowing they were close to their goal gave them energy, and they ran across the grass toward the dark tunnels.

Once they got there, they stood for a moment, looking around. They paid special attention to the clouds in the sky. Were any of them Cloud Guy?

"What do we do now?" Guy Diamond asked.

"Scream his name?" DJ Suki suggested.

"CLOUD GUY! CLOUD GUY!" they both yelled as loudly as they could, cupping their hands around their mouths and turning in every direction. "CLOUD GUY!"

"Hey," a voice said casually, "what's with all the screaming?"

CHAPTER SEVEN

Guy Diamond and DJ Suki turned toward the voice just in time to see Cloud Guy stroll down the side of a tree. He was wearing his usual striped white gym socks and calm expression.

Guy hesitated. On the trip from Troll Village, he'd been too busy dodging Zapperzines and Pinchmallas to think about what he'd say when he finally found Cloud Guy. It felt awkward to just walk up and accuse someone of stealing rainbows. "Um, well . . . ," Guy said.

"Looking for the tunnel to the Troll Tree?" Cloud Guy suggested helpfully. "The only one that doesn't lead to CERTAIN DEATH . . . death . . . death . . . death . . . ?"

"No," Guy said. "That's not it."

"Thinking about chartering a Caterbus?" Cloud Guy asked. "I've been known to drive one now and then."

"No," Guy said, shaking his head. "That's not it, either. We were just wondering if you, well . . . if by chance . . . or possibly accident . . . you might have . . ."

"Did you steal the rainbows?" DJ Suki asked bluntly, pointing her finger at him.

Cloud Guy looked shocked. "What? Steal?

Me? No, of course not!" Then he looked confused. "What rainbows?" He sat and patted the grass. "Come on. Sit down and tell me all about it."

So Guy Diamond and DJ Suki sat on the soft green grass and told Cloud Guy about the Trolls' Rainbow Rave, and how it had been ruined by someone stealing all the rainbows.

"Early this morning," Guy said, "our friend Karma saw someone dragging the rainbows away."

"It wasn't me," Cloud Guy said, shrugging. "I haven't seen a rainbow in days—weeks, even!"

"Then why did Karma see someone who fits your description?" DJ Suki asked. "Fluffy and puffy, with skinny arms and legs!"

"Hey, my arms and legs aren't that skinny!" Cloud Guy protested. "I've been working out. Look!" He bent his right arm and strained and grunted until a tiny muscle popped up. He put his arm down, breathing hard. "Did she mention handsome?"

"No," Guy said.

"Then it couldn't have been me!" Cloud Guy insisted with a toothy grin, opening his arms wide. "I mean, come on! Look at me!"

"Well," she said, "if you didn't take the rainbows, Cloud Guy, then who did?"

Cloud Guy thought about it, plucking blades of grass and tossing them in the air. "That's a good question. Who took the rainbows? Who took the rainbows . . . ," he muttered to himself.

All of a sudden, he seemed to think of something. He snapped his fingers. *SNAP!*

"I've got it!" he announced proudly. "Did the rainbow thief have a long black mustache? And a beard?"

Guy and DJ Suki glanced at each other, unsure.

"We don't know," DJ Suki said.

"Karma said she only caught a quick glimpse of him walking away with the rainbows," Guy explained. "And she only saw him from the back. So she wouldn't have seen his mustache and beard, if he had them."

Folding his blue arms across his fluffy white chest (or possibly chin), Cloud Guy looked smug. "Oh, I'm pretty sure he had them. And I think I know who stole all the rainbows!"

Guy and DJ Suki looked surprised. "Who?" they blurted at the same time.

"Evil Cloud Guy," explained Cloud Guy.

"Evil Cloud Guy?" DJ Suki echoed. "Who the heck is Evil Cloud Guy?"

Cloud Guy stretched out on the grass, supporting his head with one arm and using the other to pick more grass and toss it in the air. Several blades got stuck in his fluff, but he didn't seem to care.

"Evil Cloud Guy," he said slowly, "is this guy who looks just like me, except he's got a black mustache and beard. And instead of being cool and fun and helpful, he's evil. If you saw him from the back, you might totally mistake him for me."

Guy Diamond nodded, taking in the new information. He guessed that it made sense. Sort of. "Does he call *himself* Evil Cloud Guy?"

Cloud Guy nodded. "Oh, yeah! He's *proud* of being evil! That's his thing—being totally evil! And he's very good at it." He looked around and lowered his voice. "He's kind of a jerk, if you want to know the truth."

"And so you think this Evil Cloud Guy stole the rainbows," DJ Suki said.

"You bet! I mean, it makes perfect sense! Everybody's looking forward to seeing all the pretty rainbows in the sky, but then this meanie steals them! What could be more evil than that?

The more I think about it, the more I'm sure that Evil Cloud Guy's your thief. Case closed!" He brushed his hands together, mystery solved.

"Where is Evil Cloud Guy?" Guy asked.

Cloud Guy shrugged. "Who knows? He could be just about anywhere."

Guy was frustrated to hear that. How were they supposed to get the rainbows back from Evil Cloud Guy if they didn't know where he was?

"Well, if you had to guess," said Guy, "where would you *guess* Evil Cloud Guy is?"

"Hmm," Cloud Guy said, thinking. "I *suspect* that Evil Cloud Guy is in the evil version of the spot we're in right now."

DJ Suki stood up. She'd had enough of lying

around in the grass. Her legs were starting to itch. "Where is that? Can you take us there?"

Cloud Guy looked nervous. He bit his lip. "To get to the evil version of this spot, we'd have to go through the Increasingly Dark Forest!" Then his face relaxed into his usual calm expression. "But sure—I could take you there! No problem!"

Guy and DJ Suki didn't much like the sound of the Increasingly Dark Forest. But Cloud Guy didn't seem at all scared by it, so they figured it must not really be all that bad.

Cloud Guy popped up onto his feet and started walking. Guy and DJ hurried after him, surprised by his sudden action.

"Don't you want me to high-five you first,

or fist-bump you, or give you a hug?" Guy Diamond asked.

Cloud Guy stopped in his tracks. "Huh? Why would I make you do that?"

"Well, Branch said that's what you made *him* do!"

Grinning, Cloud Guy said, "Oh, right. Gloomy Gus. I was just messing with him—you know, for fun. Come on, let's go! Before you know it, we'll be in the"—he made his voice sound deep and scary, with an echo at the end—"Increasingly Dark Forest . . . Forest . . . forest . . . forest!" Then he switched back to his normal voice. "It sounds a lot worse than it is."

CHAPTER EIGHT

At first, the woods they walked through seemed normal, and Guy started to wonder if Cloud Guy had been joking about the Increasingly Dark Forest. It didn't seem particularly evil. But it did smell bad. Even the flowers.

"Phew," Guy said, waving his hand in front of his nose. "Maybe this should be called the Increasingly *Stinky* Forest!"

"I don't smell anything," Cloud Guy said.

"Maybe that's because you don't have a

nose, Cloud Guy," DJ Suki pointed out.

"Oh, yeah!" Cloud Guy said brightly. "That's probably it!"

They walked along in silence for a while.

"How far is it to Evil Cloud Guy?" Guy asked.

"Who?" Cloud Guy asked.

"Evil Cloud Guy," DJ Suki said. "The guy you told us about. The one we're going to see because he stole the rainbows."

"Oh, yeah," Cloud Guy said. "I was having such a nice time going for a walk with you, I forgot all about him. It's not too far. Hey! To make the time pass, maybe we should play a game!"

Guy and DJ Suki exchanged a look. Cloud

Guy didn't seem to be taking the mission to capture the thief and retrieve the rainbows very seriously. Was it all just a big joke to him? Was there even an Evil Cloud Guy? Or was he just making the whole thing up to mess with them, like he'd messed with Branch?

Could it be possible that Cloud Guy *was* Evil Cloud Guy? That he liked putting on a fake mustache and beard so he could get away with stealing stuff?

"What kind of game?" Guy asked.

"Um . . . good question," Cloud Guy said. "What kind of game . . . Let's see. . . . Oh! How about I Spy?"

DJ Suki jumped over a fallen branch. "How do you play I Spy?"

"So easy," Cloud Guy said. "I'll pick out something we can all see and give you clues. Then you try to guess what it is."

"Okay, fine," Guy said.

"Great!" Cloud Guy said. He looked up and down, scanning the woods for a good thing to spy for the game. Then he smiled. "Okay! I spy, with my little eye, something with great big sharp teeth."

ROOOAAARRR!

A big creature with a huge mouth full of great big sharp teeth jumped out from behind a tree, filling the path behind them. It looked as though it could eat five Trolls in a single bite!

"Oh—way to ruin the game!" Cloud Guy complained. "Now *anyone* can guess what I spied. Where's the fun in that? Hey, I think I should get another turn—"

SNAP! The beast snapped its teeth, lunging at the Trolls and Cloud Guy.

"RUN!" DJ Suki yelled unnecessarily, since all three of them were already running away from the creature as fast as they could.

"I *told* you this forest gets increasingly dark!" Cloud Guy said as they ran.

"JUST KEEP RUNNING!" DJ Suki shouted.

ROOOOAAARRRR!

The beast jumped forward, trying to catch Cloud Guy in his mouth, missing him by inches. Cloud Guy was so scared, he turned dark gray and started to rain. *SPLATTER! DRIP! DROP!*

As he ran and rained, Cloud Guy turned the

dirt path to mud. And that was lucky, because the big-toothed creature began to slip and sink into the mud. It yipped and yelped.

YIP! YIP! YEEP!

The creature turned around and clambered its way back to a dry section of the path. Then it shook itself, twisting its furry body and sending mud splattering against the trunks of the dark trees. The monster took one last look at the running Trolls and Cloud Guy and roared.

ROOOOAAARRR!

Then it stomped off back to the tree to wait for more victims to come along. Or possibly take a bath. And a nap.

"That thing's not chasing us anymore," Guy said, breathing hard. "It was a good idea, Cloud

Guy, making yourself rain so the path would be muddy."

"Yeah," Cloud Guy said evasively. "Making myself . . ."

Looking ahead, DJ Suki spotted a clearing that looked familiar.

"Look!" she cried, pointing. "Up there! It looks just like the meadow by the escape-route tunnels. Except . . . darker."

She was right. For every tree near the tunnels, there was a darker, shaggier, scarier-looking tree up ahead. For every bush, there was a nasty-looking bush. There were tunnel openings, but they were much darker than the ones that led to the old Troll Tree, with sharp, jagged rocks sticking out of their cold, stony walls.

Even the clouds in the sky over the clearing appeared stormy and menacing, like a thunderstorm was about to begin at any moment.

"Looks like the place!" Cloud Guy said cheerfully.

CHAPTER NINE

It took just a couple of minutes to reach the evil clearing. Guy Diamond was the only bright, shiny object in the gloomy surroundings. He and DJ Suki walked slowly, looking around for Evil Cloud Guy.

They saw no one.

"So where is he?" DJ Suki asked. "Where's this Evil Cloud Guy?"

"How should I know?" Cloud Guy said, picking his teeth.

"You said he'd be here!" Guy Diamond said.

"I said he *might* be here," Cloud Guy corrected him. "Or that he'd *probably* be here. Actually, I forget what I said."

Guy frowned. "All I know is I don't see a guy who looks like you with a black mustache and a beard, and I don't see the missing rainbows. We've come all this way for nothing!"

Cloud Guy patted the air with his blue hands. "Okay, calm down. Did you think Evil Cloud Guy would just be standing here with all the rainbows, waiting for us to come and catch him?"

Guy Diamond looked at his feet. Actually, that was pretty much exactly what he'd been thinking. Or at least hoping.

"He's undoubtedly lurking somewhere, scheming in his dark lair," Cloud Guy explained. "That's what evil dudes do."

DJ Suki took a couple of steps toward the entrances to the shadowy tunnels. "Should we start searching these tunnels?" she asked. "Maybe he's hiding in one of them."

Cloud Guy put a hand on her shoulder. "Uh, no. I don't think we should start poking around in those tunnels. That's just asking for trouble. As in, CERTAIN DEATH! Death . . . death . . . death . . ."

Guy Diamond studied Cloud Guy's face, trying to get a good read on his intentions. Was he stalling? Would he go off and disappear, then come back wearing a fake mustache and beard, pretending to be Evil Cloud Guy?

DJ Suki put her face close to Cloud Guy's. "Then what do you suggest? What are we supposed to do?"

Cloud Guy smiled calmly. "We won't go to Evil Cloud Guy. We'll get Evil Cloud Guy to come to us."

Guy Diamond looked confused. "How are we supposed to do that?"

"Well," Cloud Guy said confidently, flicking his fingers and lacing them behind his head, "lucky for you, I know exactly how to coax Evil Cloud Guy out of hiding."

"And how is that?" DJ Suki asked skeptically.

Cloud Guy looked around. He beckoned to

DJ Suki and Guy Diamond with a finger. They moved closer to him, and the three of them leaned into a huddle, putting their heads together.

"He can't resist a chance to be evil," Cloud Guy whispered. "That's his weakness. Okay? Since we know that, we can use it against him."

"How?" Guy Diamond whispered back.

"Listen and learn," Cloud Guy said, straightening. In a loud voice, he said, "Oh, look! A sweet little kid's drawing! He spent all morning drawing it! He's SO proud of his drawing! It sure would be a terrible shame if someone ripped it up!"

He stood still, waiting.

For a moment, nothing happened.

Then, up in the sky, they heard chuckling.

They looked, and saw a cloud sprout legs and walk down a tree. He was the same size as Cloud Guy. In fact, he looked exactly like him—except for his black mustache and short black beard.

Evil Cloud Guy.

"It's him," DJ Suki hissed.

"I guess Cloud Guy was telling the truth," Guy Diamond whispered.

Evil Cloud Guy looked around for the child's drawing he'd heard Cloud Guy talking about. But when he saw Cloud Guy, he walked right up to him and stood there, facing him.

"So," he growled, "it's you."

"So," Cloud Guy said, "it's me."

They circled each other with their hands out, ready for anything.

"Where's the drawing?" Evil Cloud Guy snarled, his eyes narrowing.

"What drawing?" Cloud Guy asked innocently.

"You know perfectly well which drawing I mean," said Evil Cloud Guy. "The one you were talking about. The one by the sweet little kid, that he spent all morning making. Where is it?"

"Oh, *that* drawing!" Cloud Guy said. "Funny thing about that drawing. Turns out it wasn't a drawing at all. It was a leaf." He stopped circling Evil Cloud Guy and bent to pick up a leaf from the ground. "This leaf, as a matter of fact."

Evil Cloud Guy stared at him. "You mistook a leaf for a child's drawing."

"Yup."

"That he spent all morning on."

"Uh-huh."

"And that he was really proud of."

"Correct."

Evil Cloud Guy looked disgusted. "If it were anyone else, I'd say that was ridiculous. But because it's you, I believe it."

Cloud Guy smiled. "Thank you!"

DJ Suki had heard enough of this talk about a drawing that didn't even exist. She ran up to Evil Cloud Guy and pointed at him. "Why did you steal the rainbows?" she said.

Sneering, Evil Cloud Guy slowly turned and looked DJ Suki up and down. "And just who are you supposed to be?"

"I'm not *supposed* to be anyone," she said,

shrugging. "I *am* DJ Suki."

Evil Cloud Guy raised his eyebrows. Then he laughed. "Ha, ha, ha, ha!"

Guy Diamond stepped up next to his friend. "What's so funny? She asked you a question! Why did you steal the rainbows?"

"Who are you, Sparkle Nose?" Evil Cloud Guy asked, giving Guy Diamond a withering look.

Guy folded his arms across his chest, matching DJ Suki's pose. "I'm Guy Diamond," he said in his strongest voice. "The Troll who's asking you why you stole the rainbows!"

Putting his hands behind his back, Evil Cloud Guy took a couple of slow steps away from Guy and DJ Suki. "Well, I'd never heard that Trolls are so rude. You barge into my evil clearing without knocking or saying hello. Then you accuse me of being a thief! Without the slightest shred of evidence, I might add."

Cloud Guy noticed something. "Um, excuse me, but you've got something in your fluff." He reached over to the back of Evil Cloud Guy's head and pulled out a small, colorful scrap. He held it up for all to see.

"Look at those colors!" DJ Suki cried.

"Red, orange, yellow, green, blue, indigo, and violet," Cloud Guy observed. "In that order."

"That's a piece of rainbow!" Guy Diamond exclaimed. "Where'd you get it?"

"Gimme that!" Evil Cloud Guy snapped,

snatching the striped scrap out of Cloud Guy's hand. "That's not a piece of rainbow! It's a piece of . . . gum!"

"Fine," Cloud Guy said. "Chew it."

Evil Cloud Guy looked at the colorful fragment in his hand. Then he looked at the others, who were staring at him, waiting. He popped the scrap into his mouth.

PTOOEY! He spat it out onto the ground. "Yuck! Who knew rainbows tasted so bad?"

"Rainbows!" Guy Diamond said accusingly. "AHA! I *knew* it! Where are they? What have you done with them?"

Evil Cloud Guy began to slowly back away. "I have no idea what you're talking about."

Then he turned and ran!

CHAPTER TEN

"After him!" DJ Suki shouted. Again, this was unnecessary, since Guy Diamond and Cloud Guy had started chasing Evil Cloud Guy the second he took off.

Guy had thought Evil Cloud Guy would run straight into one of the dark tunnels, but he didn't. Instead, he ran deeper into the Increasingly Dark Forest.

True to its name, it got increasingly darker.

For one thing, it got so dark that DJ Suki was glad Guy Diamond was super glittery; otherwise, she might not have been able to see to follow him as he pursued Evil Cloud Guy.

The temperature kept dropping. It got colder and colder as they went deeper into the woods. Running helped keep them warm.

The wind howled and blew into their faces, and their long Troll hair was blown straight back behind them. They couldn't whip it forward to wrap around a branch if they tried.

"STOP!" Guy Diamond shouted into the roaring wind. "Come back here, Evil Cloud Guy!" But his only answer was an evil laugh as he kept running beneath the gloomy trees, which were bent low over the path.

"I agree with the shiny dude!" Cloud Guy said, breathing hard. "Stop! I like working out as much as the next guy, but this is WAY too much running."

"Where's he going, anyway?" DJ Suki asked.

"I've got a feeling he's going to lead us straight to the stolen rainbows!" Guy Diamond shouted. Evil Cloud Guy ran around a bend in the path.

"Keep up with him!" DJ Suki said. "Don't let him get away!"

Guy Diamond pushed himself to run even faster. But when he reached the bend, he saw . . .

The path ahead was empty! Evil Cloud Guy was nowhere in sight. Guy Diamond stopped running.

WHUMP! WHUMP! DJ Suki and Cloud Guy bumped into him.

"Oops!" DJ Suki said.

"Sorry!" Cloud Guy said.

DJ Suki looked at the empty path. "Hey, where'd he go?"

"I don't know," Guy said. "It's like he just disappeared." He turned to Cloud Guy. "Is that possible? Can Evil Cloud Guy disappear?"

Cloud Guy shrugged. "I don't know. I've never seen him do it, but maybe he's been practicing."

"Wait a minute," DJ Suki said, looking at the ground. "What's this?"

Behind a rock, there was a big hole.

"Is it a tunnel?" Guy asked, peering in.

"Nope," Cloud Guy said. "Not a tunnel. That is a hole."

The three of them stood around the hole, looking into it. They couldn't see very far.

"Evil Cloud Guy could definitely fit in there," DJ Suki said. "HEY!" she yelled into the hole. "ARE YOU IN THERE, EVIL CLOUD DUDE?"

Silence.

"I guess one of us could go into the hole and look," Guy Diamond suggested, though he didn't much like the idea of jumping into a dark hole in the ground.

Cloud Guy quickly touched his nose. "Not it!" he declared.

"Maybe we should all go together," DJ

Suki said. They stood at the edge of the hole, thinking. No one was enthusiastic about the idea of going down into a dark hole. But they didn't want Evil Cloud Guy to get away, either.

"Hey, do you hear that?" Cloud Guy asked.

"Hear what?" Guy asked.

"Down in the hole," Cloud Guy said. "I hear something. Like something's . . . coming."

They each took a step back from the hole. They all could hear it now. Something was moving under the ground, sliding against pebbles and clumps of dirt. Then—

A long, colorful creature slithered out of the hole, headfirst. Its big mouth was wide open!

GRAAAARRRRRGH!

"It's a Coilencrawler!" Guy cried. "And it's

the biggest one I've ever seen!"

"The biggest one ANYONE'S ever seen!" DJ Suki yelped.

More and more of the orange-and-yellow beast emerged from the hole. And riding on its patterned back was . . . Evil Cloud Guy!

"Ha!" he cried triumphantly. "Say hello to my great big hungry friend!"

GRRROOORRRGH!

"No thanks!" Cloud Guy said. "Sorry, guys, but you're on your own with this one! I'm outta here!"

He turned around and ran back the way they'd come, as fast as his skinny blue legs could carry him.

The Coilencrawler lunged at Guy and DJ

Suki. They leapt out of the way and took off down the path, going the opposite direction from Cloud Guy.

They were headed deeper into the Increasingly Dark Forest.

CHAPTER ELEVEN

Guy Diamond and DJ Suki could hear the Coilencrawler coming after them, with Evil Cloud Guy on its back, laughing.

"Should we hair-swing?" Guy asked as they sprinted along the rocky path.

DJ Suki looked up at the branches of the trees lining the path. They were gnarled and crooked, covered in webs and slime.

"I don't think so," she said. "I don't want my

hair anywhere near those branches. We'd just get stuck. And I'm pretty sure Coilencrawlers can climb trees!"

The Coilencrawler was gaining on them, getting closer and closer. . . .

GRRRROOAAARRRGGH!

"We can't outrun that thing," Guy said. "Eventually it's going to catch us!"

"You're right," DJ Suki admitted. "And I don't think it wants to be friends!"

"I've got an idea," Guy said. He started rubbing his hands together furiously, building up a ball of glitter. "But I'll need to use your hair as a sling."

"No problem!" she said.

"Okay," said Guy, "when I say 'now,' we'll

jump off the path and get behind the biggest rock we can find. Got it?"

"Got it!"

GRRRROOOOAARRRGII!

As they ran, Guy scanned the woods ahead for a rock big enough for them to hide behind. He soon spotted one off to the right.

"NOW!"

Guy and DJ Suki jumped off the path and hid behind the rock.

From his perch atop the Coilencrawler, Evil Cloud Guy smiled a thoroughly evil smile. "Fools!" he sneered. "You think you can hide from me so easily. I saw where you went! Come out from behind that rock—or we'll come and GET YOU!"

"Fine!" Guy said from behind the rock. "Come and get us!"

Evil Cloud Guy shrugged. "If that's what you want. HEE-YAH!" He dug his heels into the Coilencrawler's orange-and-yellow sides, urging it forward. It slithered off the path and toward the rock.

GRRRAAAAUGH!

When Guy heard the Coilencrawler draw within range, he popped up from behind the rock. His glitter ball was in the sling he'd made with DJ Suki's hair. "EAT GLITTER, COILEN-CRAWLER!" he shouted as he let the ball fly.

FWAM! The glitter ball flew straight into the Coilencrawler's wide-open mouth and burst, filling its mouth with glitter!

The creature coughed and sputtered, spitting out glitter. *PTOOEY! PLAH! PLAP!*

The Coilencrawler turned away from the rock, heading back toward its hole in the ground to work on getting all the glitter out of its mouth.

"Where do you think YOU'RE going?" Evil Cloud Guy raged. "Turn around! Get back to that rock! GET THOSE TROLLS, YOU WORTHLESS TUBE OF SLIMINESS!"

He bounced up and down on the Coilencrawler, kicking it with his heels, trying to make it turn around. Still spitting out glitter, the beast bucked Evil Cloud Guy off, sending him flying!

"AAAAHHHH!" Evil Cloud Guy yelled as he sailed through the air before landing, facedown, on the path. "OOF!"

The Coilencrawler slithered to its hole, leaving a trail of gleaming silvery glitter.

Evil Cloud Guy shook his fist at the creature. "Come back here!" he yelled. "YOU'RE SUPPOSED TO BE MY EVIL FRIEND!"

"Come on!" Guy Diamond whispered to DJ Suki. "Now's our chance! Let's get him!"

They ran out from behind the rock, planning to launch themselves at Evil Cloud Guy and tackle him. But they couldn't help stepping on the sticks and twigs that covered the ground, so the villain heard them coming. He turned and sprinted down the path, heading even deeper into the Increasingly Dark Forest.

"Come back here!" DJ Suki shouted.

"No!" Evil Cloud Guy yelled without

looking back, still running. Guy and DJ Suki were growing tired, but they forced themselves to take off after him, trying not to let him out of their sight. They both felt they'd come way too far to give up now.

Before too long, though, the path ended. They caught glimpses of Evil Cloud Guy, but they had no idea where he was leading them.

"Where's the path?" DJ Suki asked. "Are we going the right way?"

"I'm not sure," Guy admitted. "There really isn't a path anymore. But I just saw Evil Cloud Guy a second ago, right by that toadstool up there. Come on!"

Guy led the way to the toadstool Evil Cloud Guy had passed a moment before. But now the plants around them were close together, with thick, thorny stems. Guy couldn't see very far ahead.

And he couldn't see Evil Cloud Guy anywhere.

"Do you see him?" Guy asked DJ Suki.

She shook her head. "Maybe if we're quiet for a moment, we'll hear him," she suggested. They stood still, listening to the wind and the strange sounds of unseen animals. They couldn't hear anything that sounded like Evil Cloud Guy's footsteps. But then they heard his evil laugh.

"Heh, heh, heh, heh . . ."

"That way!" DJ Suki whispered, pointing.

They carefully moved through the sharp plants in the direction of the laughter. DJ Suki kept getting her clothes caught on the spikes and thorns, but they managed to slowly press forward. Then, right in front of them, they saw a low tunnel made of brambles and briarwood. By getting down on the ground and crawling, they could enter it.

Guy didn't hesitate. He crawled into the thorny tunnel, inching forward. He felt sure Evil Cloud Guy had come this way. DJ Suki followed right behind him.

They crawled for what seemed like a long time, but it was hard to measure distance in the dark, twisting tunnel. Suddenly, the tunnel ended at a round chamber, where they were able to stand up and look around. The chamber was a dome made of sticks and branches tightly woven together. The sticks were covered in sharp thorns.

Evil Cloud Guy wasn't there.

"What is this place?" DJ Suki said.

"I don't know," Guy answered. "Maybe it's where Evil Cloud Guy lives."

"Then where is he?" DJ Suki asked. "And where are the rainbows?"

WHAM! Behind them, a slab of stone dropped in front of the tunnel, blocking their way out. The Trolls ran to the stone and tried to slide it aside, but it was way too heavy and wouldn't budge.

Then they heard a familiar laugh.

"Heh, heh, heh, heh," Evil Cloud Guy chuckled from somewhere outside the chamber. "How do you like my little trap?"

CHAPTER TWELVE

"I DON'T like it!" DJ Suki shouted. "Let us out of here! RIGHT NOW!"

Evil Cloud Guy only laughed more. "Heh, heh, heh. No, I don't think so. I think I'll leave you right there. You know, all that running made me hungry. I'll go have a nice meal. Goodbye."

DJ Suki and Guy heard the sounds of Evil Cloud Guy walking away. Guy peer through the gaps between the sticks and branches, but they were too narrow. He couldn't see much of anything. Besides, the chamber was dark and shadowy. Still, he kept working his way around it, trying to find a weak spot, or at least a place with a bigger peephole. When he got almost back to where he'd started, he saw something.

"Colors!" he said, surprised. He turned to DJ Suki. "Come here! Look at this!"

She hurried over and peered through a gap in the tightly woven limbs. It was hard to see in the gloom, but she saw a quick flash of color. She gasped. "Is it . . . the rainbows?"

Guy nodded. "I think so. Maybe Evil Cloud Guy is keeping the stolen rainbows in another trap right next to us! We've got to get out of here and set the rainbows free!"

"Agreed," DJ Suki said. "But how?"

"I don't know," Guy admitted.

Then they heard something. *TAP! TAP! TAP!*

It was coming from the other side of the stone slab.

"Hello?" asked a familiar voice. "Anybody home?"

It was Cloud Guy!

Guy and DJ Suki rushed over to the stone slab. "Cloud Guy!" they cried. "You came back!"

"Yeah," Cloud Guy said from the other side of the rock. "I realized I was sick of getting blamed for all the rotten stuff Evil Cloud Guy does. It's time to stand up to that bully! Or at least help you two escape from his trap."

"Thank you!" Guy Diamond said.

"No problem. Now let's move this rock. It's really in the way of you escaping."

"We tried that already," DJ Suki said. "It's too heavy."

"Hmm," said Cloud Guy. "Well, how about this? Now we've got *three* of us to move it. And remember: I've been working out! Why don't you two grab the top of the rock and pull? I'll push on it from this side, and maybe we can tip it over. Ready? One . . . two . . . three . . . PULL!"

Guy Diamond and DJ Suki grabbed the top of the stone slab and pulled with all their might. Cloud Guy pushed on the other side, grunting and straining. "ERNGH! GRUNGH! URRNGH!"

The rock started to move! Guy and DJ Suki jumped out of the way just as the heavy stone slab fell into the chamber. *WHOMP!*

"WE DID IT!" DJ Suki cheered as Cloud Guy crawled in. They all hugged.

"Okay," Cloud Guy said. "Now let's get out of here!" He got down on his hands and knees and started to crawl out of the tunnel.

"Wait!" Guy cried. "What about the rainbows? We have to get them back. And what about standing up to Evil Cloud Guy?"

"Yeah, kinda getting cold feet about that," Cloud Guy confessed, "in spite of my comfy gym socks. Let's just run back to the escape-route tunnels and call it a day." He kept crawling. Guy and DJ Suki crawled after him, all the way out of the tunnel. They got to their feet.

"Now we have to go back for the rainbows," Guy said. Cloud Guy started to protest, but Guy held up his hand. "Here's my plan. . . ."

ℓℓℓℓℓℓℓℓℓ

Evil Cloud Guy finished eating and decided to check on his prisoners. He was walking back toward the outside of his trap when he heard something strange.

Music! But not evil music. It was a happy, bouncy little tune.

"This is the Increasingly Dark Forest," he growled, "not the Happy, Bouncy Forest! Who's playing that music?"

He followed the sound. It seemed to be coming from behind a huge old tree stump. He tiptoed around the stump and then leapt forward threateningly. "AHA!" he cried.

He saw DJ Suki blowing through a leaf, playing it like a flute. She was tapping on a hollow log with her foot. The happy, bouncy tune was coming from her.

"What are you doing?" Evil Cloud Guy said, utterly mystified.

"Distracting you," DJ Suki said.

"From what?"

"Them!"

Before Evil Cloud Guy could turn around to see who she meant, Guy Diamond and Cloud Guy had sprinted around him, each holding one end of a strong vine. In a flash, Evil Cloud Guy was all tied up!

"Got you!" Guy said triumphantly.

"Let's go!" Cloud Guy said, tugging on the vine like a leash.

"Where are we going?" Evil Cloud Guy asked.

"To the rainbows," DJ Suki answered. "Lead the way!"

They found all the rainbows hidden in a chamber similar to the one they'd been trapped in. Evil Cloud Guy opened the chamber, and the others started pulling the rainbows out, releasing them into the sky.

"Why'd you do it?" Guy asked. "Why'd you steal all the rainbows?"

To everyone's surprise, Evil Cloud Guy started to cry. "I just wanted attention! I'm lonely. Nobody wants to hang out with an evil guy! I'm tired of being evil. I want to be popular!"

"What were you going to do with the rainbows?" DJ Suki asked.

"I thought maybe I could open a theme park," Evil Cloud Guy admitted. "People would come to see the rainbows, and I'd be popular."

Guy Diamond actually felt sorry for him. Then he had an idea.

eeeeeeee

Back in Troll Village, the young Trolls were looking gloomy.

"Come on!" Poppy said, trying to cheer them up. "Didn't we have fun today, playing games and singing songs about rainbows?"

"Yes," Jody said. "But it just doesn't seem like a Rainbow Rave without any rainbows."

"Look!" Biggie cried, pointing. "Up in the sky!"

Sure enough, one rainbow sprang into the sky, and then another, and another, and soon DOZENS of rainbows filled the sky with beautiful colors! The young Trolls jumped up and down with excitement, clapping and cheering. So many rainbows!

Then one rainbow stretched down from the sky and touched the ground in the main square of Troll Village. Guy Diamond, DJ Suki, Cloud Guy, and Evil Cloud Guy came sliding down it and landed right in the center of the village.

Poppy ran up to them. "Guys, you did it! You found the missing rainbows! I knew you'd do it!" They all hugged, except Evil Cloud Guy, who hung back shyly. "Um, who's that?" she whispered.

"That's our new friend!" Guy Diamond explained. "And he'd like to help with our Rainbow Rave!"

Guy asked Biggie if Evil Cloud Guy could hand out the rainbow cupcakes.

"Sure!" Biggie said. "That'd be GREAT!"

Evil Cloud Guy got to hand out the cupcakes with rainbow frosting to all the Trolls in the village. This made him VERY popular! He did not feel lonely at all.

From then on, Evil Cloud Guy was known

as Used to Be Evil Cloud Guy!

And even though the rainbows had arrived a little late, thanks to Guy Diamond, DJ Suki, and Cloud Guy, it turned out to be one of the best Rainbow Raves EVER!